Darkness and the Butterfly

Ann Grifalconi

Little, Brown and Company
Boston   Toronto

First Edition

Library of Congress Cataloging-in-Publication Data
Grifalconi, Ann.
  Darkness and the butterfly.

  Summary: Small Osa is fearless during the day, climbing trees or
exploring the African valley where she lives, but at night she becomes
afraid of the strange and terrifying things that might lie in the dark.

  [1. Fear—Fiction.   2. Night—Fiction.   3. Africa—
Fiction]   I. Title.
PZ7.G8813Da   1987   [E]   86-27561
ISBN 0-316-32863-4

Published simultaneously in Canada
by Little, Brown & Company (Canada) Limited

Printed in Italy

There is an old African saying:
"Darkness pursues the Butterfly."
This story is for all those
Who have feared the darkness. . . .

Dedicated to
My brother, JWG, and to KK,
Who helped me to find the light!

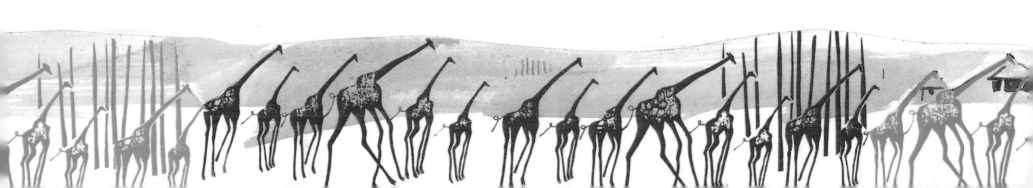

Have you ever been afraid of the dark?

Of being alone in the night

When strange things float by

That seem to follow you . . .

With eyes that glow in the darkness?

NOT TOO LONG AGO, nor far away,

Where spirits live in the trees and rocks

And in the animals that roam at night,

There was a bright and pretty girl named Osa

Who was *so* afraid of the dark . . .

No matter what her mother or grandfather said

When evening came

Osa would not leave the house.

She would sit in the corner

Hugging her knees to her chin

And her eyes would grow big and black with fear.

And she would stay that way
Refusing food and comfort 'til she fell asleep.
Then her mother would lift her gently
And tuck her into bed.
Wishing she could find some way to show Osa
Not to fear — but to know the beauties of the night.

Yet during the day . . .

Osa was afraid of nothing she could see

For while Osa was very small, she was, oh, so lively,

She could climb anything THREE TIMES her size . . .

Even the big Baobab Tree!

Osa was very curious, too,

And each day, she spent hours

Exploring every part of the valley where they lived.

She loved to bring home the special things she found:

Some pretty wildflowers for her mother

A bright leaf or bird's feather for her grandfather.

Or just some colored stones to keep.

But when nighttime fell . . .

Fearless Daytime Osa

Became just as fearful as before!

She would not stop trembling

Even when her mother gave Osa a chain

Of bright red worry beads to comfort her.

Then her loving mother sighed and wondered . . .

Would Osa *never* give up her fear of night?

ONE AFTERNOON

When Osa had been wandering about the valley

Looking for some more colored stones

She lost her way!

Osa sat down to think for a minute,

Listening to the wind

And holding onto her Mama's beads for comfort —

Then suddenly, sparkles of light dazzled her eyes!

Osa stood up, shielding her eyes with her arm,
And saw that the sunlight reflected from some bottles
Stuck on almost every branch of the trees
That surrounded a bright pink house on the hill ahead!
Then Osa knew where she was:
Those were the "bottle trees" of the Wise Woman.
Her Mama had told her *that* was how she made sure
The friendly ancestor spirits who lived in the trees
Would stay and protect her home.

Everyone said the Wise Woman knew so many things:

How to find wild herbs to heal sick people;

And even . . . how to explain your dreams!

Just then a yellow butterfly fluttered past Osa,

Flying to the dazzling light of the bottle trees.

Osa ran after it, toward the house on the hill.

The Wise Woman was standing outside
Sorting some fragrant leaves into piles.
Osa asked if she could help. The Wise Woman smiled:
"You can help me dry these herbal tea leaves."
She showed Osa how to thread the leaves upon a string.
Then she helped Osa climb a ladder
And hang the strings of herbs from the roof poles,
To dry in the clear mountain air.
Working together all afternoon like that,
They soon became friends.

Finally they sat down to rest and drink some tea.
The Wise Woman saw that Osa was getting sleepy
From being out in the hot sun,
So she lifted Osa onto her lap.
Stroking her soft brown hair, she said,
"You've been so nice to help me, Osa,
And so brave to go up that tall ladder!"
Osa hung her head.
"I'm not so brave — not all the time — not at night!"

When she thought about the darkness
Osa could feel a shiver go through her.
The Wise Woman felt it and hugged her close.
"Oh, I know how you feel, Osa!
I grew up here in the woods, and sometimes,
When I was alone, I used to get scared, too —
Specially at night!"
Osa clutched the Wise Woman's hand.
"It's just that . . . darkness *hides* everything!

"There are Spirits, *hungry* Spirits
Wandering about in the dark of night!
They could *catch me* with their long legs —
Grab me with their long, slippery fingers —
Stare at me with their burning eyes!
And then . . . They would EAT me!
You see," Osa whispered, "I could *never* run fast enough!
I am so small . . . the SMALLEST of the small!"

The Wise Woman smiled and shook her head,
Pointing to the yellow butterfly fluttering nearby,
Warming its brightly colored wings in the waning sunlight. . . .
"But look at that little butterfly, Osa,
She must think SHE is the smallest of the small . . .
Darkness pursues her, too —
Yet *she* flies on!"

Sleepily, Osa thought about that.

"Maybe she has a secret?"

Then she shook her head.

"But I have no wings to fly . . . . !"

Then Osa heard the Wise Woman's soft voice:

"You will find your own way. . . . You will see."

Osa nodded, and before she knew it,

She fell into a deep sleep.

Osa dreamed that the yellow butterfly flew by
Shining brightly — as if it carried its own light inside.
Brushing Osa's cheek with its soft wings,
It seemed to say: "Follow me. . . . Follow me!"

Osa got up and ran after the little butterfly
Whose bright wings beat a path through the darkness
But Osa felt something grab her shoulder
And she turned about quickly!

It was only a little branch —
But she had lost the brave light of the butterfly.
She was all alone. . . .
Osa lay down upon the ground and cried.

Osa felt the warmth of the earth beneath her. . . .
It was only then Osa felt something inside herself
Changing. . . . She was growing lighter!

She was floating up through the air like the butterfly,
Flying along with the moon
High in the night sky over her village!

Then she looked about her
And saw that the night was not really
Dark at all!

It was filled with the twinkling lights
Of a thousand friendly stars
And the radiant light of the moon. . . .

Then Osa woke up. . . .

She was still in the lap of the Wise Woman,
Who was smiling down at her now.
Osa looked up, remembering her dream —
Still filled with such a great and happy feeling.
Then Osa told the Wise Woman all about her dream.

Just as Osa finished, saying,
". . . . *and there was light everywhere!*"
The yellow butterfly flew by
And lit fearlessly — right on the palm of her hand!
Osa looked at it, holding her breath.
"Maybe I can be as brave as she is?"
The Wise Woman nodded.

Then the Wise Woman took Osa's hand in hers.

"Now it's your time to fly, Osa — it's getting dark!

Time for you to fly on home!" She paused.

"Do you want me to walk with you?"

Osa shook her head.

"No . . . I think I can go by myself this time

I know my own way now."

Suddenly realizing what she herself had said,
Osa laughed out loud and jumped down
From the Wise Woman's lap.
"I'm not afraid anymore!"

The Wise Woman stood up then,
Smiling down at her new friend.
Osa hugged her good-bye, promising,
"I'll be back to visit again, soon . . . you'll see!"

Then Osa raced home . . . as fast as a butterfly!
And even though it was quite dark
Osa found her own way —
Past the bottle trees, down the valley,
All the way to her village . . .
And she was not afraid!

WHEN OSA got home,

She was so excited she couldn't wait:

"Mama! Mama!

I can be just as brave as the butterfly . . . SEE?

I'm not afraid of the dark anymore!"

Her mother looked at Osa — It was true!

. . . It was dark and Osa was not afraid!

At that, she grabbed Osa's hands
Then she and Osa began to laugh happily together
Until the whole family joined in!

And that is how it came about
That Osa — the smallest of the small —
Found the way to carry her own light through the darkness
For all the days and nights of her life to come!

JP
Grifalconi, Ann
Darkness and the Butterfly:
$14.95

51801